Library of Congress Cataloging-in-Publication Data
Reynolds, Adrian.
Pete and Polo's farmyard adventure / by Adrian Reynolds.—lst ed.
p.   cm.
Summary: When Pete and his polar bear, Polo, visit Grandpa on his farm, they help find ten missing ducklings.
ISBN 0-439-30913-1 (alk. paper)
[1. Ducks—Fiction. 2. Farm life—Fiction. 3. Grandfathers—Fiction. 4. Polar bear—Fiction. 5. Toys—Fiction.] I. Title.
PZ7.R33215 Pg 2002   [E]—dc21   2001035073

10 9 8 7 6 5 4 3 2 1   02 03 04 05

Printed in Hong Kong/China
First edition, May 2002

Pete and Polo's Farmyard Adventure

Adrian Reynolds

ORCHARD BOOKS • NEW YORK

An Imprint of Scholastic Inc.

To Eileen

Pete and Polo were down on the farm with Grandpa.

The best thing about staying at Grandpa's
was riding around on the toy tractor.
It was green and red, and it had a trailer
and pedals to make it go.

One morning Grandpa took Pete
and Polo through the meadow to the
duck pond.

"There are lots of new little ducklings down there," he said.

But when they got there,
the ducklings were gone.

"Oh, dear," said Grandpa.
"It's been so hot that the duck
pond has dried up."

Poor little ducklings,
thought Polo.

"How many ducklings were there, Grandpa?" asked Pete.

"Hmm, let me see," said Grandpa. He thought for a moment. "Ten, altogether," he said.

"Don't worry, Grandpa," said Pete, "we'll find them for you." And off they set.

"The ducklings must be feeling very thirsty," said Polo.

Pete had a feeling this was going to be their best adventure yet.

The very first place they came to was the kennel, and there, splashing around in Buffy's water bowl, were two fluffy yellow ducklings.

"You were right, Polo," said Pete. "They must all be looking for water."

"Quack! Quack-quack!" agreed the ducklings.

Pete and Polo carefully put the two little ducklings into the trailer and set off to find the others.

They soon found another three ducklings, splashing around beneath the old water pump over by the barn.

"So now we have one . . . two . . . three . . . four . . . five ducklings in all," said Polo.

"But where are the others?" asked Pete.

"I bet they'll be somewhere where there's water, too," said Polo.

And Polo was right.
They found another
duckling cooling off
in Grandpa's
watering can . . .

. . . and another one, sitting on her
own under the drippy old tap.
"One . . . two . . . three . . .
four . . . five . . . six . . .
seven ducklings,"
counted Polo.
"Only three left."

Two more ducklings were swimming around in the pigs' water trough, and Pete and Polo found the very last one . . .

. . . in the water bucket.

"Hooray!" cried Polo. "That's ten altogether—we've found them all!"

"Let's take them back to the farmhouse," said Pete.

Pete and Polo parked the tractor outside the kitchen door.

"You stay here and look after the ducklings," said Pete, "while I go and tell Grandpa."

Polo looked at the ten little ducklings. The ten little ducklings looked back at Polo. They were very, very hot. "Hmm," said Polo.

Pete found Grandpa down by the duck pond. He was filling it with water.

As they ran up to the house, Pete told Grandpa how he and Polo found the ten little ducklings.

But when they got back,
Polo and the ducklings had vanished!

"Oh no, Grandpa!" cried Pete.
"Now we have to start all
over again, and this time
we'll have to find Polo, too!"

But just then Grandpa heard a
splishy-splashy sound coming from
the kitchen. He looked through
the window.

"Ho! ho!" he laughed. "I don't
think we have to look far for
them, Pete! Come and see!"

"Quack! Quack-quack!"
said the ten little ducklings.
"Quack!" agreed Polo.

Grandpa filled the trailer with water,
and Pete and Polo drove back down to the
duck pond, with the ten little ducklings splashing
and sploshing happily behind.

That evening, as the sun went down, they all watched the ducklings swimming happily in the duck pond. Pete and Polo both agreed that finding the ten little lost ducklings was their best adventure yet.